FRIENDLY

Titles in this Series:

Afraid	Happy
Angry	Hurt
Brave	Jealous
Confident	Lonely
Friendly	Sad

Copyright © text 1994 Steck-Vaughn Company

Library of Congress Cataloging-in-Publication Data
(Revised for vols. 7, 8, 9, 10)
Amos, Janine.
    Feelings.
       Contents: [7] Brave – [8] Confident –
[9] Friendly – [10] Happy
       1. Emotions–Case studies–Juvenile
literature. [1. Emotions. 2. Conduct of
life.] I. Green, Gwen, ill. II. Title.
BF561.A515 1994   152.4   90-46540
ISBN 0-8172-3775-5 (v. 1)
Originally ISBN listed as 0-8172-3775-5
   Afraid ISBN 0-8172-3775-5 (v. 1): Angry ISBN 0-8172-3776-3 (v.2);
Hurt ISBN 0-8172-3777-1 (v. 3); Jealous ISBN 0-8172-3778-X (v. 4);
Lonely ISBN 0-8172-3779-8 (v. 5); Sad ISBN 0-8172-3780-1 (v. 6)

New titles are listed as: Brave ISBN 0-8114-9228-1 (v. 7); Confident
ISBN 0-8114-9229-X (v. 8); Friendly ISBN 0-8114-9230-3 (v. 9); Happy
ISBN 0-8114-9231-1 (v. 10)

Editor: Deborah Biber
Electronic production: Alan Haimowitz
Printed in Spain
Bound in the United States
1 2 3 4 5 6 7 8 9 0 LB 98 97 96 95 94 93

FRIENDLY

By Janine Amos
Illustrated by Gwen Green

RSVP
RAINTREE
STECK-VAUGHN
PUBLISHERS
The Steck-Vaughn Company

Austin, Texas

EMILIO'S STORY

David and Emilio had been to swimming practice. Emilio was hungry. He was thinking about his dinner. It might be spaghetti and meatballs. That was his favorite. Just then David stopped.

"Hurry up," said Emilio.

"I've lost my watch," said David.

Emilio groaned. "We can't go back now—it's too far. And we're nearly home."

David didn't move. "That watch cost a lot of money. I can't go home without it. My mom'll kill me!" said David.

Emilio laughed. "Don't be stupid!" he said. But he thought that David's mom might shout. She did get pretty mad sometimes.

"Hold on! I may have put my watch in here," said David. He threw down his bag. Emilio watched his friend take everything out of the bag. Soon David's trunks, his soap, and his wet towel were lying on the pavement. A dog sniffed at them.

"Let's try your bag," said David. So Emilio shook his towel, trunks, and soap onto the pavement too. They found some chips in the bag. But there was no watch.

"Have you checked your pockets?" asked Emilio.

David checked them all—twice.

"It's no use," he sighed. "It's lost."

How do you think David feels?

It was windy, Emilio started to feel cold. He began to think about his dinner again. David was packing his bag very slowly. Emilio jumped up and down to keep warm.

"Your mom will phone the pool right away," said Emilio. "Your watch will be safe."

"I don't want to go home without it," David said again. He looked really worried.

What could Emilio do to help?

Emilio had an idea.

"I know," said Emilio, "I'll come home with you. It's better with two. And your mom won't be so mad if you've got a friend with you."

"Great!" said David.

The two boys ran all the way to David's house.

How is David feeling now?
How do you think Emilio is feeling?

David's mom was in the kitchen.

"Hello, you two!" she said as the boys walked in.

"She doesn't look angry," thought Emilio. But you could never be sure with David's mom.

"Hi, Mom," said David in a quiet voice. He was glad that Emilio was standing next to him.

"Here goes!" thought Emilio.

Just then David ran to the table. He could see something lying there. It was something belonging to him. It was his watch! Quickly, David picked it up.

"You forgot to wear your watch this morning," said David's mom. "It's just as well—you might have lost it at the pool."

David gave Emilio a huge grin.

"Can Emilio stay for dinner, Mom?" asked David.

"Of course he can," smiled David's mom. She turned to Emilio.

"Do you like spaghetti and meatballs?" she asked.

Feeling like Emilio

Emilio was cold and hungry. He wanted to go home for his dinner. But he stayed to help David instead. Have you ever been friendly like Emilio?

Someone else

Being friendly means thinking about someone else. Pretend to be the other person just for a minute. Think how he or she might be feeling. Is there anything you can do to help?

Friends

Friends can share a problem. They can't make the problem go away. But they can talk about it—and make the problem seem smaller. Sometimes friends can help just by being around.

Think about it

Read the stories in this book. Think about the people in them. Do you feel like them sometimes? Think how people have been friendly to you. How can you be friendly to others?

RACHEL'S STORY

Rachel was having a party. She was keeping it a secret. Only Rachel's best friend Jane knew. They were making the party invitations together. "It will be a secret party—until the invitations are ready!" laughed Rachel.

But Jane didn't keep the secret. She told Anna. And pretty soon the whole class knew.

"You've spoiled my surprise," cried Rachel.

"I didn't mean to," said Jane, staring at her feet.

"You promised not to tell," Rachel said. "I always keep your secrets."

Jane turned red. "I'm sorry," she said.

Rachel was mad. "I don't like you anymore!" she shouted.

After school, Rachel ran right past Jane. She joined up with some other girls.

"Hey! Wait for me!" Jane called.

"I'm not talking to you!" shouted Rachel. "And you're not coming to my party!"

"I don't want to come to your stupid party!" shouted Jane. But she didn't look happy. She looked as if she might cry. Rachel was pleased.

Why do you think Rachel was pleased?
How do you think Jane feels?

When Rachel got home she slammed the door behind her. Her mom was reading a newspaper.

"I'm fed up with Jane," said Rachel. She told her mom what had happened.

"Jane's not coming to my party," said Rachel. "And I'm not talking to her ever again."

"Hmm," said Rachel's mom. "Jane shouldn't have broken her promise. But she's your best friend. Can't you forgive her?"

"No!" said Rachel.

Do you think Rachel should forgive Jane?

Later Rachel got out the party invitations. They were almost ready. Rachel finished the coloring. She started to fill in the names. It wasn't so much fun making them without Jane. Rachel found Jane's invitation and scribbled on it with a black marker.

Rachel looked at the ruined invitation. She felt sad. She remembered Jane calling her party "stupid." But that didn't make Rachel feel any better. "I wish Jane hadn't told," Rachel thought. "I wish she was still my friend."

Rachel's mom sat down next to her. "Cheer up, Rachel," she said.

"Who's your best friend, Mom?" Rachel asked.

"Your dad, I suppose," said Rachel's mom. "And Aunt Pauline."

"I bet Aunt Pauline doesn't break her promises," said Rachel.

"She does sometimes," said Rachel's mom. She looked a little annoyed. "In fact Aunt Pauline promised to come over to help me with your party. But today she telephoned me. She's going on vacation instead."

Rachel put down her marker. She looked at her mom.

"Will you forgive her?" Rachel asked. She liked Aunt Pauline.

"Yes," replied Rachel's mom. "Pauline and I have some good times together." Rachel's mom smiled. "Sometimes our friends do things we don't like. We get upset with them, but they're still our friends."

Is Rachel's mom right?

At bedtime Rachel was still busy.

"It's time for bed, Rachel," said her mom. "What are you doing?"

"I'm making another invitation," said Rachel, yawning. "It's for Jane."

"I thought you weren't friendly with Jane any more?" said Rachel's mom.

"I'm forgiving her," said Rachel.

Why has Rachel changed her mind?

Feeling like Rachel

Have you ever felt like Rachel? Has anyone ever made you so mad that you shouted, "I don't like you?" Perhaps you didn't really mean it. You just meant that you didn't like what they'd done.

Talking about it

Sometimes our friends upset us. They hurt us by the things they say or do. They've forgotten to think about our feelings. Then we have to remind them and talk about it. We have to tell them how we feel—or they won't know. There's no need to stop being friends.

ADAM'S STORY

The group of boys stood in the playground. Tom had a plan.

"Let's go to the park after school," he said. "We can try that new tactic!"

"I'll be trainer!" shouted Steve.

Adam was pleased. They could use his new soccer ball. He gave it a bounce.

Adam saw someone watching them. It was the new boy in the class. He was standing by himself in the playground. Adam wondered if the new boy wanted to play. But Tom was already racing away.

"Hurry up!" called Tom.

Adam didn't want to be left behind.

"See you!" he waved to the new boy. Adam ran off after his friends.

After the game Adam went home for dinner. Adam's dad and his big brother Jason were there.

"I made a save today," said Adam.

"Who did you play with?" asked Adam's dad.

"Tom and Steven and the others," answered Adam. Then he told his dad about the new boy at school.

"Did he go to the park with you?" asked Adam's dad.

"No," said Adam.

"I bet he felt left out," said Jason.

"Tom didn't ask him to come," Adam said.

"Who cares?" said Jason. "You could have asked him."

Is Jason right?

Jason put down his comic.

"You were only a baby when we moved here," he told Adam. "You don't remember being new. But I do. I didn't know anyone. It was horrible."

"But you've got lots of friends!" said Adam.

"I have now," said Jason.

Adam was interested. "How did you make friends?" he asked.

"I took my comic collection into school," said Jason. "I was reading it on my own. One boy asked if he could have a look. Then some of his friends came over. There was a big group. Soon I knew lots of kids."

Adam thought for a while.

"But why didn't you go over to the boys?" he asked his brother. "Why did you have to wait?"

"It was hard to do that," said Jason. "Those guys all knew each other. I was the odd one out."

"I know what Jason means," said Adam's dad. "I remember being new here, too. It took me a long time to make friends."

"What happened?" asked Adam and Jason together.

"I remember feeling lonely," said Adam's dad, "especially at lunchtimes. I sat eating my lunch by myself. So I did the crossword puzzle."

"And what happened then?" asked Adam.

"One day someone asked me to the cafeteria. I met lots of other people. Now I go there every lunchtime." Adam's dad laughed, "That's why I'm so fat!"

"Being new sounds awful!" said Adam. "I'll ask the new boy to play soccer tomorrow."

"That would be a friendly thing to do," said Adam's dad.

The next day at school Adam ran up to his friends. He couldn't wait to join in the game. Then Adam remembered the new boy.

"Hi!" he called. "I'm Adam."

"I'm John," the new boy called back. And Adam kicked him the ball.

After the game the boys crowded around John. They wanted to know all about him. They had lots of questions to ask.

Adam looked at John and the rest of the group. "It's sort of like my brother's story," he thought.

How did Jason's story help?

Making friends

It's hard to be friendly if you're new. Everyone else knows each other. You feel all alone. So what Adam did was important. He helped John to be part of the group.

Friends' welcome

Have you ever been friendly, like Adam? Have you ever welcomed a new boy or girl into the group? If you have, you know that it's a good feeling. It's a very good feeling to be welcomed, too!

Needing a friend

We all need a friend sometimes. And there's always someone else who needs a friend. Are you good at being friendly? Who's been friendly to you?

Being a friend

Think about the stories in this book. Emilio, Rachel, and Adam each learned different things about friendship. What have you learned? How many ways can you show that you're a good friend?

If you are feeling frightened or unhappy, don't keep it to yourself. Talk to an adult you can trust:
- one of your parents or other relatives
- a friend's parent or other relative
- a teacher
- the principal
- someone else at school
- a neighbor
- someone at a church, temple, or synagogue

You can also find someone to talk to about a problem by calling places called "hotline." One hotline is **Child Help**, which you can call from anywhere in the United States. Just call

1-800-422-4453

from any telephone and stay on the line. You don't need money to call.

Or look in the phone book to find another phone number of people who can help. Try
- Children and Family Service
- Family Service

Remember you can always call the Operator in any emergency. Just dial 0 or press the button that says 0 on the telephone.